CARTER HIGH
M Y S T E R I E S

WHERE IS
Mr. Zane?

By Eleanor Robins

SADDLEBACK
EDUCATIONAL PUBLISHING

CARTER HIGH
M Y S T E R I E S

SADDLEBACK
EDUCATIONAL PUBLISHING
www.sdlback.com

Copyright ©2006, 2011 by Saddleback Educational Publishing

ISBN-13: 978-1-61651-569-0
ISBN-10: 1-61651-569-4
eBook: 978-1-61247-137-2

Printed in Guangzhou, China
NOR/0813/CA21301539

17 16 15 14 13   3 4 5 6 7

Chapter 1

Jack sat at the bus stop. He was talking to his friend, Logan.

Both boys had Mr. Zane for science. And they had a test today.

Jack asked, "Did you study for the science test?"

"Yeah. After I got home from rehearsal," Logan said.

Logan was in the school play. And he had the best part.

"I studied a lot for the test. So I should do okay on it," Logan said.

Drake slowly walked up to them. All three boys lived at Grayson Apartments.

And all three were good friends.

Logan asked, "What's wrong with you, Drake? Why are you walking so slowly? Did you hurt yourself at football practice?"

Drake was on the football team. He was the starting quarterback. And he had Mr. Zane for science, too.

"No. I'm just tired," Drake said.

"Why? Didn't you sleep well, Drake?" Jack asked.

"I slept okay. But I stayed up too late. I had a lot of homework," Drake said.

"You must have studied a lot for our science test. I did, too," Logan said.

Jack had studied a lot for the test, too. But he didn't stay up late to do it.

"I didn't study for the science test, Jack," Drake said.

That surprised Jack. "Why?" Jack asked.

"Yeah, Drake. Why? Did you forget we

have a test today?" Logan asked.

"No. But I didn't have time to study for it. I had too much history homework. And I can't get any more bad grades in that class. So I had to do all of that homework first," Drake said.

"But what about your science test?" Jack asked.

"I hope I'll do okay on the test. But I'm not sure I will. So I'm worried about taking the test," Drake said.

Jack was glad he'd studied. Or he would be worried about taking the test, too.

Drake said, "I wanted to study for the test. But I was too tired when I finished my history homework. And I knew it wouldn't help to study then."

"Maybe you can study on the bus," Jack said.

"I will. But I need to study more than

that," Drake said.

Jack knew Mr. Zane always gave hard tests. So Drake needed to study a lot.

Drake asked, "Do you think the test will be hard?"

"Mr. Zane's tests are always hard," Logan said.

"That's for sure," Jack said.

Drake said, "Maybe Mr. Zane will be out today. And we won't have the test. Then I can study tonight."

"Mr. Zane would never be out on a test day," Jack said.

"Yeah, Drake. You can forget about that," Logan said.

"You never know. He might be out today. I can always hope that he will be," Drake said.

"You can hope all you like, Drake. But Mr. Zane will be there. He would never be out on a test day. That's for sure," Jack said.

Chapter 2

Jack was in his first class. He was thinking about Drake. Jack was worried about him. He hoped Drake did okay the science test.

The bell rang. Jack was glad the class was over. He hurried out of the room. Jack went to look for Drake. Jack wanted to know how Drake thought he did on the test.

Jack looked for Drake. But he didn't see him. Some students came out of Mr. Zane's class. All of them were talking. Jack had never heard students talk that loudly in the hall before.

Jack thought they must be talking about the test. Jack hoped that didn't mean that the test was very hard.

Drake came out to the hall. He didn't seem upset. So Jack thought he must have done okay on his test. Jack hurried over to him.

"How was the test? Do you think you passed?" Jack asked.

"We didn't have the test," Drake said.

That surprised Jack very much. Mr. Zane had never called off a test before.

"Why?" Jack asked.

"Mr. Zane didn't come to class. Mr. Glenn was our teacher," Drake said.

Mr. Glenn was the principal.

"Mr. Glenn didn't know where the test was. So he couldn't give it to us. Now I can study tonight. And I won't fail the test," Drake said.

"I'm glad for you, Drake. But why

isn't Mr. Zane here?" Jack asked.

Logan hurried over to them before Drake could answer Jack.

"How was the test?" Logan asked.

"We didn't have the test," Drake said.

Logan seemed very surprised. "Why?" he asked.

"Mr. Zane didn't come to school this morning," Jack said.

"He didn't? Why? Is he sick?" Logan asked.

Drake said, "Mr. Zane called Mr. Glenn. He told Mr. Glenn he would be late to school. But he didn't tell Mr. Glenn he would be late to class."

"Why didn't Mr. Glenn know Mr. Zane would be that late?" Logan asked.

Drake said, "Yeah. Teachers have to be here before we do. And he said he would be here in time for his first class."

"I can't believe Mr. Zane isn't here.

I studied a lot for nothing last night," Logan said.

"But it's good you studied. You'll still have to take the test tomorrow," Jack said.

"Yeah. But that means I have to study again tonight," Logan said.

Drake said, "It's hard to believe Mr. Zane isn't here. He gets upset when students are out on a test day. So it's hard to believe he's out on a test day."

Jack said, "That's true. Do you think something happened to him?"

"No. He must have had some trouble with his car. And it took longer to fix it than he thought it would. So that's why he's late," Logan said.

"But he could have called back. And he could have told Mr. Glenn that he would be late to class," Drake said.

"But maybe the car broke down on the way to school. And he couldn't call again," Jack said.

"Mr. Zane could use his cell phone," Drake said.

Logan said, "We're talking about Mr. Zane, Drake. And you know he doesn't like cell phones. He's told us that more than one time."

"That's for sure," Jack said.

"Oh, yeah. I forgot about that." Drake said.

Mr. Glenn came to the door of Mr. Zane's room. He said, "All students need to get to class. It's almost time for the bell to ring."

"We'd better get to class now," Jack said.

Logan said, "I know I had better get to class. I have Mr. Zane next. So Mr. Glenn is my teacher now."

"Maybe Mr. Zane will come soon. And you can take your test," Jack said.

"I hope he will. I want to get this test over with. I don't want to study for it again tonight," Logan said.

Logan hurried into Mr. Zane's room.

Jack said, "I'll see you at lunch, Drake."

Then Jack hurried to his next class. Jack wanted to take his science test. So he hoped that Mr. Zane got to school before his science class. But most of all, he hoped that Mr. Zane was all right.

Chapter 3

Jack had a lot of work to do in his next class. So he didn't have time to think about why Mr. Zane was late to school.

Then the end of class bell rang.

Jack wanted to find out if Mr. Zane had come yet. So he hurried out of the room. And he walked down the hall.

Jack saw many students. They were in front of Mr. Zane's door. Mr. Zane might have arrived. But Jack didn't think he had yet.

Then Jack saw Logan. He hurried over to Logan.

"Did Mr. Zane arrive?" Jack asked.

"No. He didn't. I'll have to take that test tomorrow. And I'll have to study again tonight," Logan said.

Jack might have to take the test the next day, too. But he wasn't worried about when he would have to take the test. He was worried about Mr. Zane.

"Did Mr. Zane call Mr. Glenn again?" Jack asked.

"No. Mr. Glenn hasn't heard from him again. I think Mr. Glenn might be worried about Mr. Zane. Or he might be upset with him," Logan said.

Drake hurried over to them.

"Did Mr. Zane get here yet?" Drake asked.

"No," Logan said.

"Did he call again?" Drake asked.

"No," Logan said.

"Is Mr. Glenn upset that he didn't arrive?" Drake asked.

Logan said, "I don't know about Mr. Glenn. But I'm upset that I have to study for the test again."

"You should be worried about Mr. Zane. Something might have happened to him," Jack said.

"Don't worry about him, Jack. He'll be here tomorrow. And he might make the test twice as hard," Logan said.

Jack didn't think Mr. Zane would do that. And he thought the two boys were joking. But he wasn't sure. Sometimes he knew when they were joking. But he didn't always know.

Mr. Glenn came to the door of Mr. Zane's room. He said, "All students need to get to class."

Jack thought Mr. Glenn seemed upset. Was he upset with the students? Or was Mr. Glenn just upset because Mr. Zane wasn't there yet?

"We'd better get to class. See you later," Logan said.

"Yeah," Drake said.

Logan and Drake started to walk quickly down the hall. And Jack hurried to his next class.

Chapter 4

Jack's next class went by fast. And then it was time for his science class.

Jack hurried to Mr. Zane's room. Many students were talking outside Mr. Zane's door. So Jack knew Mr. Zane hadn't got there yet.

Mr. Glenn came to the door of Mr. Zane's room.

Mr. Glenn said, "Don't stand around in the hall, students. You need to get to class."

The other students started to leave. And Jack hurried into Mr. Zane's room. Levi came in. He went to a desk next to

Jack and sat down. Levi was in two of Jack's classes. And he was also on the football team. The bell rang to start the class.

Levi asked, "Where is Mr. Zane? Why isn't he here?"

"Yeah?" some other students asked.

Some of the students started talking to each other. Mr. Glenn just looked at them. And he didn't say anything. Then students got very quiet.

Mr. Glenn said, "I don't know where Mr. Zane is. He called this morning. And he said he would be a little late to school. But he said he would be here in time for his first class."

"So why isn't Mr. Zane here?" Levi asked again.

"I don't know," Mr. Glenn said.

Jack asked, "Did Mr. Zane tell you when he'll be here?"

"No, Jack," Mr. Glenn said.

"Mr. Zane should be here. We have a test today," Levi said.

"I know that, Levi," said Mr. Glenn. "But you'll take the test tomorrow."

"I studied a lot last night. And that isn't fair," Levi said.

"I don't have a copy of the test. So you can't take it today," Mr. Glenn said.

Jack wasn't worried about the test. He was worried about Mr. Zane.

Jack said, "Mr. Glenn, I'm worried about Mr. Zane. He might need to be out on a test day. But he would tell you he would be gone all day."

"Maybe Mr. Zane knew he would be gone all day. And he didn't want to tell Mr. Glenn," Levi said.

But Jack didn't believe that.

Mr. Glenn said, "Mr. Zane didn't know he would be out all day. Or he would have left a copy of the test."

"That's for sure," Jack said.

Jack thought Mr. Glenn should call the police. Jack asked, "Did you call the police, Mr. Glenn?"

At first Mr. Glenn didn't answer Jack. And it seemed as if he didn't want to answer Jack.

But then Mr. Glenn said, "Yes, Jack. I did."

"Are the police looking for Mr. Zane?" Jack asked.

"No, Jack," Mr. Glenn said.

"Why? They should be looking for him," Jack said.

"Yeah," some other students said.

"The police said Mr. Zane hasn't been missing very long. They said it's too soon to look for him right now," Mr. Glenn said.

Levi asked, "Mr. Zane is missing? I thought he just wanted to take a day off from school."

Mr. Glenn said, "I shouldn't have said Mr. Zane is missing. He's only late to school."

"Very late," Levi said.

But Jack thought Levi believed Mr. Zane just wanted a day off. And he thought most of the students believed that, too.

But Jack didn't believe that. And Jack thought Mr. Glenn also believed that Mr. Zane was missing.

Something must have happened to Mr. Zane. But what? Where was Mr. Zane? Was he okay?

Chapter 5

Later that morning, Jack hurried into the lunchroom. He got his lunch. Then he looked for his friends.

He saw Logan and Drake. They sat at a table. Willow was with them.

Jack hurried over to the table and sat down with his friends.

Willow said, "I heard Mr. Zane didn't come to school this morning. Now we can't have our science test. You had his class just before lunch, Jack. Did Mr. Zane ever come to school?"

"No," Jack said.

Drake said, "I hoped Mr. Zane would

be out today. But I didn't think he really would be. But I'm glad he is."

"I'm not glad. I'm very worried about Mr. Zane," Jack said.

"Why? Didn't Mr. Zane call Mr. Glenn again?" Logan asked.

"No. Mr. Zane didn't call Mr. Glenn again. And I'm very worried about him," Jack said.

"Don't worry about him, Jack. I'm sure Mr. Zane is all right," Willow said.

"I think you are wrong, Willow. I think something's happened to Mr. Zane," Jack said.

"Why do you think that, Jack?" Logan asked.

"Yeah. Why do you think that?" Drake asked.

"I think that Mr. Zane is missing," Jack said.

"Missing?" Logan asked.

"Yes. Missing," Jack said.

"Why?" Willow asked.

"Yeah. Why? He's only late to school," Drake said.

"Mr. Glenn must be worried about Mr. Zane. He told us that he'd called the police," Jack said.

The other three seemed very surprised at what Jack just said.

"Are the police looking for Mr. Zane?" Logan asked.

"No," Jack said.

"Why aren't they? Don't they think he's missing?" Drake asked.

Jack said, "The police said Mr. Zane hasn't been missing that long. He has to be missing for longer before they will look for him."

"How much longer?" Logan asked.

"I don't know. Mr. Glenn didn't say," Jack said.

Paige and Lin came over to the table and sat down.

Paige said, "I heard Mr. Zane didn't come to school today."

"I heard that, too," Lin said.

"Why?" Paige asked.

Jack told them what he had just told the other three. Then Jack said, "I'm very worried about Mr. Zane."

Logan said, "School isn't over yet. So Mr. Zane could still come to school."

"Right," Drake said.

"Maybe," Jack said.

But Jack didn't believe that. He was really sure something had happened to Mr. Zane.

"I think someone should look for Mr. Zane. He might be in trouble. And he might need help," Jack said.

"Don't worry, Jack. Mr. Zane is okay," Willow said.

"Yes, Jack. I'm sure that Mr. Zane is okay," Lin said.

"Yeah," Logan said.

"Yeah," Drake said.

"But how do you know Mr. Zane is okay?" Jack asked.

No one had an answer for that.

Paige said, "I'm worried about Mr. Zane, too."

"Why are you worried about him, Paige? You don't have him for science," Logan said.

"So? I can still worry about him. He isn't here. And Mr. Glenn doesn't know why he isn't here," Paige said.

"I think we should do something," Jack said.

"I think Jack is right. I think we should do something," Paige said.

"Do what?" Logan asked.

"Yeah. Do what?" Drake asked.

Willow said, "Don't worry, Jack. Mr. Zane could still get to school today. Or he could call Mr. Glenn."

"But what if he doesn't? And what if he doesn't call?" Jack asked.

"Then the police will look for him," Logan said.

"Yeah," Drake said.

But Mr. Zane might need help before then. And the police might be too late to help him.

Chapter 6

The end of school bell rang.

Jack hurried out of his classroom. And he walked to the bus. He saw Mr. Glenn. Jack hurried over to talk to Mr. Glenn.

Jack asked, "Mr. Glenn, did you hear from Mr. Zane?"

Mr. Glenn seemed very worried.

"No, Jack. I didn't hear from him," Mr. Glenn said.

"Did you call the police again?" Jack asked.

Mr. Glenn said, "Yes, Jack. I did. I called them just before school finished."

"Are they going to look for Mr. Zane

now?" Jack asked.

"Not today, Jack. The police think Mr. Zane will come to school tomorrow. Or maybe he'll call me," Mr. Glenn said.

"But what if he doesn't come tomorrow? And what if he doesn't call you?" Jack asked.

"Then the police will look for him. But there isn't a thing they can do today," Mr. Glenn said.

But Mr. Zane might need help today. Jack knew there wasn't a thing he could do at school. So he hurried to the bus.

Jack was glad when he got home. He put his backpack in his apartment. Then he went outside. And he sat on the steps.

Jack was very worried about what might have happened to Mr. Zane. Maybe Jack could think of something he could do to help him.

Paige and Lin walked over to Jack.

They sat down on the steps.

"Did you hear anything else about Mr. Zane?" Lin asked.

"No. Did you?" Jack asked.

"No. I'm sure he's okay," Lin said.

But Jack didn't believe that. And he didn't think Lin did either.

"Do you think Mr. Glenn will call the police again?" Paige asked.

Jack said, "Mr. Glenn called the police again, just before school finished."

"What did the police say? Are they going to look for Mr. Zane?" Lin asked.

"The police think Mr. Zane will come to school tomorrow. Or maybe he'll call Mr. Glenn," Jack said.

"But what if he doesn't call?" Paige asked.

"The police will look for him then," Jack said.

"So the police will look for Mr. Zane

tomorrow? But not today?" Paige asked.

"Yes. And I'm worried about him. He might need help now," Jack said.

Lin said, "Don't worry, Jack. I'm sure he's okay."

Paige said, "You might be sure about that, Lin. But I'm not sure about that. And I think we should do something."

"What? Just say the word. And I'll do it," Jack said.

"I think we should look for Mr. Zane. And I think we should do it right now," Paige said.

Lin said, "I don't think we should do that, Jack. I think we should let the police do their job."

"But they won't look for him until tomorrow," Paige said.

"That's right, Lin. And we need to do something now," Jack said.

"Yes. We do," Paige said.

"What should we do first, Paige?" Jack asked. "I think we should go over to Mr. Zane's house. And we should make sure he isn't there," Paige said.

"I'll drive us over to his house," Jack said.

Jack was the only one who had a car. So he was always ready to drive them somewhere.

"Okay. I think we should go now," Paige said.

"I don't think we should go over there," Lin said.

"Then don't come with us, Lin," Paige said.

"I think someone should make sure that you don't get into trouble. So I'll go," Lin said.

Paige said, "Good. Now I need to tell someone where I'm going."

"Me, too. I'll meet you at my car in ten

minutes," Jack said.

"Okay," Paige said.

"Okay," Lin said. But Lin didn't sound as if she wanted to do it.

Chapter 7

Ten minutes later, the three were in Jack's car. And they were ready to go.

Jack and Paige were in the front seat. Lin was in the back seat. Paige had her cell phone in her hand.

"What do you have in your hand, Paige?" Jack asked.

"I pulled up a map of the city on my phone. I thought we might need it," Paige said.

"Good idea," Jack said.

Logan yelled to them. "Wait." He ran over to the car. "I just got home from rehearsal," Logan said. "Where are you going?"

Paige said, "To look for Mr. Zane. Do you want to go with us?"

"Sure. Why not?" Logan asked. Logan opened the car door. And he got into the back seat with Lin.

Jack started the car. Then he pulled out into the street.

"I'm still not sure this is a good idea," Lin said.

"Someone has to look for Mr. Zane," Paige said.

"Where are we going first?" Logan asked.

"To Mr. Zane's house. We want to make sure he isn't there," Paige said.

"Good idea. Do you know where he lives?" Logan asked.

"Yes," Paige said.

"How do we get there?" Jack asked.

Paige looked at her phone. Then she

told Jack how to get there.

They drove for a while. And then they got to Mr. Zane's house.

The garage door was open. Jack saw Mr. Zane's car. It was parked in the garage.

Paige said, "Look. Mr. Zane's car's in his garage."

"Yeah. Maybe he's home," said Jack. He turned into Mr. Zane's driveway. And he stopped the car.

Paige and Logan quickly got out of the car. Jack got his keys. And then he got out of the car. But Lin still sat in the car.

Paige asked, "Are you coming with us, Lin?"

"No. I'll stay in the car," Lin said.

Paige hurried to the front door. She started to ring Mr. Zane's doorbell.

Jack walked into the garage. He

looked at Mr. Zane's car. The car had a flat tire.

"Look, Logan. The car has a flat tire," Jack said.

Logan said, "That must be why Mr. Zane said he would be late to school. I wonder why he didn't change the tire."

"Maybe he didn't have a spare tire," Jack said.

Paige hurried into the garage. She said, "Mr. Zane didn't come to the door. I rang the bell ten times."

"I'm sure you did," Logan said.

Jack showed the flat tire to Paige.

"I wonder where Mr. Zane is, Jack," Paige said.

"I want to know, too," Jack said.

"Where should we look now, Jack?" Logan asked. Then Logan walked over to Jack's car.

Paige asked, "Where are you going

now, Logan?"

"To the car. You said Mr. Zane isn't here," Logan said.

"I didn't say that. I said he didn't come to the door. That isn't the same thing," Paige said.

Logan stopped walking. "Okay. So what do you want to do now?" he asked.

"Let's look around outside the house," Paige said.

"I don't know about that, Paige," Logan said.

"And I'm not sure that's a good idea either, Paige," Jack said.

Paige started to walk around the house. Jack and Logan soon followed her.

Paige looked in the windows. Then she yelled Mr. Zane's name.

They got to the back of the house. Jack heard a noise. Logan heard it, too.

"What was that noise? And where did

it come from?" Logan asked.

"I don't know," Jack said.

Jack heard the noise again. But what was it? And where did it come from?

Chapter 8

Jack heard the noise again.

Paige walked over to some bushes next to the house.

"Where are you going now, Paige?" Logan asked.

"Yes, Paige. Where are you going now?" Jack asked.

Paige pushed between two bushes. Then Paige got down on the ground. She said, "I see a window down here. It must be a basement window."

Jack heard Paige knock on the window a few times.

"Be careful, Paige. Don't break the

window," Logan said.

Jack heard the noise again. Then Jack heard Paige knock on the window a few more times.

Jack heard the noise again. Paige stood up. Then she said, "I think Mr. Zane made that noise. And I think he's in the basement."

Paige came out from behind the bushes. She said, "Come on. We're going into the house."

Lin came up behind them. She said, "What are you doing back here? I think we should go."

Jack said, "We think Mr. Zane is in the basement."

"And we're going into the house to look for him," Paige said.

"Yeah," Logan said.

"I don't think that's a good idea," Lin said.

"Then stay out here," Paige said.

"Yeah," Logan said.

"How will you get into the house?" Lin asked.

Jack wondered the same thing. He wanted to find out if Mr. Zane was in the house. But he didn't want to break into the house.

"Maybe a door is unlocked," said Paige.

"But what if a door isn't unlocked? What will you do then?" Lin asked.

"Call the police," Jack said.

"Yeah. I think they would come since we heard a noise," Logan said.

Paige tried the back door. But the door was locked. Paige went to the front door. The other three followed her there.

Paige tried the front door. But the door was locked, too. Then Paige went into the garage. The other three did, too.

Jack saw a door that went from the garage into the house. Paige tried to open the door. The door opened.

"Come on," Paige said.

Paige went into the house. Jack and Logan followed her.

Lin said, "I'll wait out here."

"Mr. Zane. Mr. Zane," Paige yelled.

Logan said, "Stop yelling, Paige. Or we won't be able to hear Mr. Zane."

"That's for sure," Jack said.

Then Jack heard a noise. It was the same noise he heard outside.

Logan said, "I heard that noise again. Where did it come from?"

"Mr. Zane. Where are you?" Paige yelled.

Jack heard the noise again. Jack went over to a door.

"I think it came from behind this door," Jack said.

Paige quickly opened the door. Some steps were on the other side of the door. The steps went down to the basement.

Paige started walking down the steps. Jack and Logan were behind her.

Jack saw Mr. Zane. He was on the floor, near the window. Some big shelves were lying on top of him. And he couldn't get up.

The three hurried over to Mr. Zane.

Mr. Zane said, "It's about time someone came to see about me."

"Are you all right?" Jack asked.

"I hurt my leg. I think it might be broken," Mr. Zane said.

Paige said, "Mr. Zane might really have a broken leg. So don't move him. I'll go upstairs and call for help."

The boys started to move the big shelves off Mr. Zane.

"How did the shelves fall on you, Mr. Zane?" Jack asked.

"Yeah. And why are you down here?" Logan asked.

"My car has a flat tire," he said.

"Yeah. We saw it. But why are you down here?" Logan asked.

"I wanted to get something out of the basement. I needed it to change my tire. But I didn't want to be late to school. So I was in a hurry. And I knocked the shelves over," Mr. Zane said.

The boys got the shelves off Mr. Zane. But they didn't move him.

Then Logan said, "We didn't have our test today, Mr. Zane. Does that mean we won't have to take a test on that chapter?"

Then Logan laughed. Jack didn't think that was funny.

Mr. Zane looked at Logan. And he didn't seem pleased.

Mr. Zane said, "That wasn't funny.

If I don't have a broken leg, I'll be at school tomorrow. Maybe I'll make the test harder, just for you, Logan."

"That's for sure," Jack said.

"And you'd better be ready to take your test," said Mr. Zane.

Jack knew Logan was only joking with Mr. Zane. But Jack didn't think Mr. Zane knew that.

But one thing Jack did know. All of Mr. Zane's students had better be ready for their science test tomorrow.

That was for sure.